Yaya The Sheep

Super Silly, Furry, Friends

D1403864

To order additional copies of this book, contact:

Follow Yaya The Sheep
On Facebook
and
CherylCheatham.Com

ISBN: Softcover   978-1-6641-6853-4
         EBook   978-1-6641-6854-1

Print information available on the last page

Rev. date: 05/11/2021

Written and Illustrated By
Cheryl Cheatham

Dedication

Yaya The Sheep is dedicated to
my little ones who love, support,
encourage, and humor their
Yaya!

Who Do You Want To Be When You Grow Up?

A hot air balloon pilot, an author, a butterfly catcher, a pastry chef, a super hero? Join Yaya The Sheep and 19 of her super silly, furry, friends and explore 17 amazing, exciting, fun jobs.
Whatever you decide, find joy and spread love and kindness.

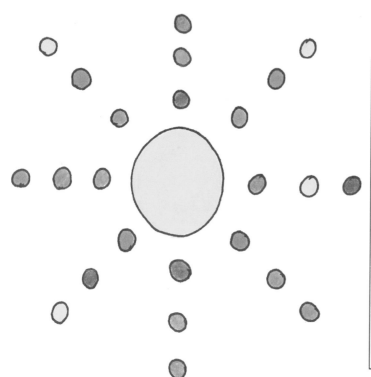

Hot Air Balloon Pilot – Hot air balloons can go up to 3,000 feet high. They can be any color, design, and fly as fast as the wind blows. Would you like to take a hot air balloon ride?

Kind Hearted

Kitty

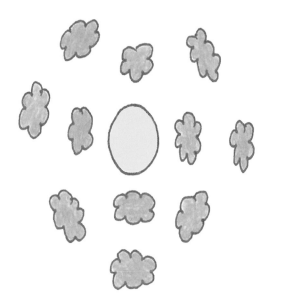

Super Hero – A super hero is courageous and helps people in need. Anyone can be a superhero. You can even wear a cape. What would be your super hero name?

Colorful Chameleon

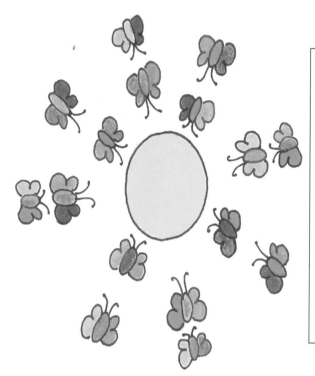

Butterfly Catcher – There are 17,500 species of butterflies. Butterflies flap their wings 5 times every second and fly about 12 miles an hour. What is your favorite butterfly color?

Peppy Puppy

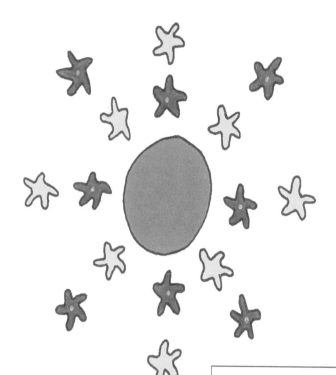

Gentle Giraffe

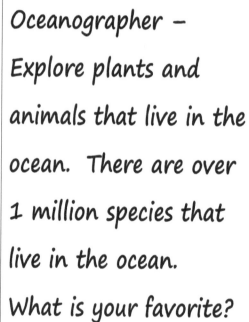

Oceanographer –
Explore plants and
animals that live in the
ocean. There are over
1 million species that
live in the ocean.
What is your favorite?

Cat Walker – Cats have 12 whiskers on each side of their face. Whiskers help cats know how close they are to objects. Cats have an average of 30 million hairs. A cat's tail is about 10" long. Have you ever owned a cat?

Pretty Miss Polly

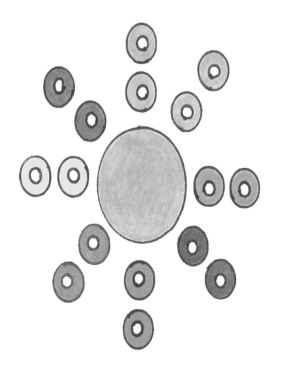

Pastry Chef – Bakes and decorates cupcakes, donuts, and pastries. There are many sizes, shapes, and flavors. The most popular flavors are chocolate, vanilla, lemon, and carrot. What is your favorite?

Pretty Polar Bear

Fire Fighter – First responder in many different emergencies. Fires, car crashes, and accidents are just a few examples. They save lives every day. They live in a firehouse when on duty and get to drive a big red truck.

Zany Zebra

Author – An author writes books about something they love. Books are a great way to learn new things, giggle at funny stories, and go on exciting adventures.

Do you have a favorite book?

Pretty Peacock

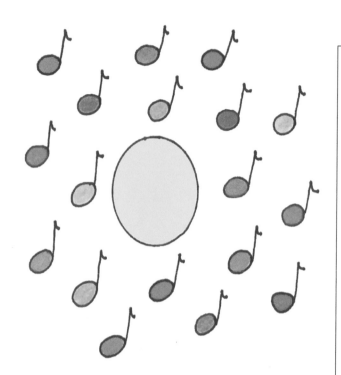

Music Teacher – Teach music and musical instruments to students. A music teacher works on plays, choir, band, and concerts. Music class is fun. What is your favorite instrument?

Darling

Dinosaur

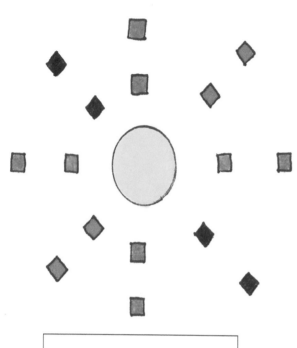

Race Car Driver – You drive cars REAL fast! You race other drivers on oval tracks, dirt tracks, and road courses. You wear a uniform, helmet, and gloves to protect you. If you win you get a checkered flag and a trophy. What color race car would you want?

Beautiful

Blue Bird

YaYa
International
Speedway

PTS
Racing

88

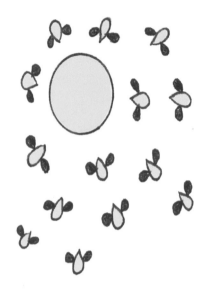

Silly Skunk

Bee Keeper – Bees pollinate flowers, fruits, and vegies. A bee hive can make 100 pounds of honey a year. What do you put honey on?

Astronaut – You can travel to outer space in a rocket. You wear a space suit, helmet, and gloves to protect you. Would you like to walk on the moon, float in outer space, and see the Earth from 238,855 miles away?

Fearless Fox and

Tough Tiger

Food Truck Owner – A food truck is a small restaurant on wheels. You order tacos, hamburgers, pizza, ice cream, and many more. Food trucks are at the beach, in the mountains, in the city, even your school parking lot.

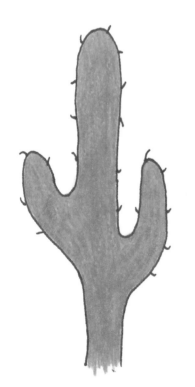

Crazy Cat

Veterinarian – A doctor for animals. You take care of them when they are healthy and sick. There are 35 kinds of animals. How many different animals have you owned?

Loveable

Lion

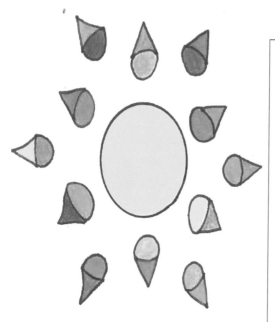

Snow Cone Maker – Snow cones are shaved ice covered in a delicious, colorful, syrup. One very popular snow cone is rainbow. They are great for a hot, summer, day. What is your favorite snow cone flavor?

Cheerful Cow

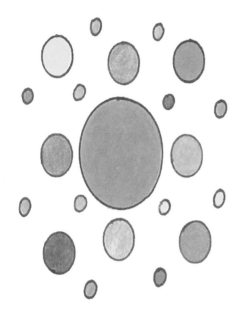

Bubble Gum Taster – There are 187 flavors and comes in many bright colors. Popular flavors are cherry, cinnamon, spearmint, and watermelon. What is the biggest bubble you have ever blown?

Happy

Hen

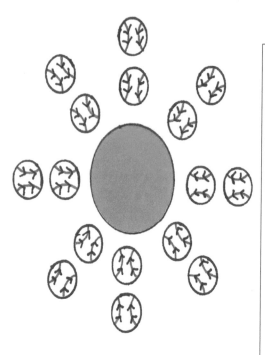

Athlete – Baseball players use balls, bats, gloves, bases, and get to wear a colorful uniform with their name on it. Baseball, football, basketball, soccer, and tennis are 5 fun sports to play. What sport do you play? Do you have a favorite athlete?

Lucky Llama

Snow Cone Maker
Vet
Cat Walker
Astronaut
Pastry Chef
Music Teacher
Hot Air Balloon Pilot
Author
athlete
Butterfly Catcher
Race Car Driver
Super Hero
Bubble Gum Taster
Bee Keeper
Food Truck Owner
Firefighter
Oceanographer

Draw Your Favorite Animal or Job

Love, Yaya The Sheep

CPSIA information can be obtained
at www.ICGtesting.com
Printed in the USA
LVHW070544260821
696111LV00001B/1